PHANTOM OUT OF TIME

Phantom Out of Time

by Nelson S. Bond

Graed Garroway's empire on Earth was toppling, smashed by the flaming vengeance of Dirk Morris who struck from nowhere with blinding speed and true justice. Yet such a thing could not be—for Dirk Morris was dead, slain at the brutal command of the Black Dictator.

Metal grated upon metal, a heavy gate at the far end of the corridor swung open, and footsteps stirred dull echoes down the quiet prison-block. Neil Hardesty turned beseeching eyes to his friend and leader.

"Dirk," he begged, "for the last time ... let us share this with you? Please!"

Vurrth, the hulking Venusian, nodded mutely, lending his support to Neil's appeal. Shaughnessey, Vurrth's earthly equal in size and strength, rumbled deep in his throat, "Yes, Dirk. We're all in this together. Let's take the punishment together ... like men."

Dirk Morris shook his head. His voice was firm; his gaze calm and steady.

"No. It's better *one* of us should die, than all. We set ourselves a righteous task: to rid the System of a madman and a tyrant. We pledged ourselves to fight ... to win ... or to die. Our first leader has already given his life that worlds may someday again breathe the air of freedom. A dozen of our comrades have paid the price of rebellion. Edwards, Johnson, Vallery ... our blood-brothers.

"Now it is my turn. But my passing does not mean we give up the fight. You, Hardesty, must take over the leadership of our little clan. When you have been freed, carry on! Find new recruits; rebuild our organization. Four against an empire is mighty odds, but if you four surrender, the liberty of all men is doomed for generations!"

Fred Meacher said hopefully, "That's right. Someone must pick up the torch. Neil, if you'd rather not, *I'll* bear the *Message—*"

"Never mind," said Hardesty. "I'm ready to take it. Well, Dirk?"

The footsteps were drawing nearer. Swiftly, coolly, but deliberately, Dirk Morris placed his lips close to Neil's ear, whispered a brief sentence. Hardesty started. His eyes first widened, then narrowed with incredulous surmise.

"Dirk!" he gasped. "But that's.... You can't mean—"

PHANTOM OUT OF TIME

"Quiet!" warned Brian Shaughnessey. "Here they come! The skulking rats!" He spat contemptuously on the floor as a band of armed men halted before the cell in which the quartet was imprisoned.

The foremost guardsmen parted, and before the grille appeared a man tall and powerful, dark of eye and beetling of brow; a personage whose innate ruthlessness and cruelty could not be disguised even by the ornate finery he wore. This was Graed Garroway, "Black" Garroway, tyrant of Earth, emperor of the System, Overlord—by force of arms—of the entire Solar Union.

He smiled. But there was little mirth in his smile, and no sincerity.

"Well, Morris?" he demanded.

"Well?" repeated Dirk stonily.

"Your time passes swiftly. Have you decided to tell your secret?"

"I know one thing," said Morris, "that is no secret. My time passes swiftly, yes. But so does yours. The days of your dictatorship are numbered, Garroway. Soon the cleansing flame of righteous rebellion will rise to sweep you and every evil thing you stand for from the face of creation!"

Garroway stiffened, flushing with dark anger.

"You speak boldly for a doomed man, Morris. Guards, open the cell!" He scowled. "It may amuse you to learn that I did not need your information, traitor. I gave you a final chance to offer it of your own free will. But your cherished 'secret' has already been solved."

"Solved!" That was Hardesty. "You mean—?"

"Quiet, Neil!" warned Dirk. "He's faking!"

Garroway laughed.

*

"Faking? You shall see in a few minutes, when I put you to death in the murderous device constructed by your one-time leader, Dr. Townsend!"

"Murderous—" began Hardesty.

"Please, Neil! Then you ... you found Dr. Townsend's chamber?" asked Dirk.

"Yes. And experimented with it, too. We know, now, its purpose. Too bad Robert Townsend did not live to receive our congratulations. So that was

6

your secret, eh? Your late leader succeeded in perfecting a disintegration chamber?"

"Disint—" began Morris. Then he stopped abruptly. When he spoke again, his voice was defiant. "Well ... now that you know, what are you going to do about it?"

Brian Shaughnessey stared at his friend miserably.

"Disintegrating machine!" he choked. "Nothing but a damned theoretical gadget! Is *that* the great invention we've been risking our lives for? Dirk—"

"Do about it?" laughed Garroway negligently. "Why, I'm going to turn it to my own usage, of course. And you, my unfortunate young conspirator, will attain the distinction of being the instrument's first human victim. Come, guards! We have no more time to waste."

"A moment!" interrupted Morris. "You will keep your promise? My companions go free when I die?"

The Overlord nodded with mock graciousness.

"Graed Garroway needs compromise with no man. But I have given my word. Yes, your companions go free."

"Very well, then. I am ready."

Morris turned and gripped warmly the hand of each of his companions in turn. Then he stepped forward. Two guards flanked him. The Captain of the Guard rasped a command. The little band marched down the avenue and out of sight; silence surged in to hush the stir of footsteps. Somewhere a barrier clanged metallically.

"A disintegrating machine!" moaned Shaughnessey. "A damned disintegrating machine! Suppose we *did* have it? What good would it do us? It wasn't portable. We couldn't use it to fight Garroway's hordes. Dirk's just thrown his life away for nothing—"

"Please, Brian!" begged Hardesty.

His hands were knotted at his sides, the knuckles as white as his lips. Meacher's eyes were ghastly. Only Vurrth displayed no emotion, but the sinews of the Venusian's throat were taut cords of strain as he, with the others, waited.

PHANTOM OUT OF TIME

Slow seconds passed on sluggish feet. Then, after a million aeons, came the dreaded signal. From afar sounded the thin, persistent hum of pulsing current; the strong lights of the prison-block dimmed briefly ... glowed ... dimmed again ... and glowed....

*

Brian Shaughnessey, strong fighting man that he was, raised a hand to his eyes. Neil Hardesty's breath broke in a shaken murmur. Meacher whimpered, and Vurrth's massive fists tensed at his thighs.

Again a door opened ... again footsteps approached the prisoners. There was a look of gloating malice on Garroway's swarthy face. He said, "Open the cell, guards. Let them out now."

Hardesty whispered, "It ... it is over?"

"It is over. Your friend has vanished ... disappeared into whatever hell awaits rebels." The Overlord smiled. "It was a most interesting exhibition ... most. Through the glazed pane we saw him standing, panic-stricken, frozen with terror. Then the current was turned on. Before our eyes, he vanished as a mist—"

"I don't believe it!" growled Shaughnessey. "Morris was afraid of nothing; man, beast, nor devil—"

"And ... *and we?*" broke in Fred Meacher fearfully.

"Go free," said Black Garroway, "as I promised. But have a care! If ever I hear a word of complaint or suspicion raised against any of you again, you will share his fate. It is only through my graciousness you live."

"We understand," said Neil evenly. "Come, friends."

He led the way from the cell as a guard unlocked the door. When the four had almost reached the end of the prison corridor, Garroway called after them.

"Oh ... one thing more! I almost forgot to thank you, Meacher!"

Shaughnessey said, "Huh? What's that? Why? What's he got to thank *you* for, Fred?"

Meacher's pale eyes rolled, suddenly panicked.

"Me? I ... I don't know what he's talking about—"

8

NELSON S. BOND

Black Garroway's heavy laughter filled the hall.

"What? Oh, come now, Meacher! Of course you do. I appreciate the information you gave me on Morris. The reward I promised you will be waiting at the State Hall tomorrow. A thousand credits, wasn't it? Well, come and claim it—" He chuckled stridently—"if you can."

Before the quick suspicion rising in the eyes of the comrades he had betrayed, Meacher quailed. He tugged free of Shaughnessey's hand and scampered to the protection of Garroway's guard. His voice bleated shrill remonstrance.

"Sire ... you should not have told them! I served you faithfully and well ... wormed my way into their inner council! Were it not for me you would never have known—"

Black Garroway avoided the informer's frenzied clawing. His voice was hard, mocking, contemptuous.

"Fool! You brought me no information worth hearing! Through my own efforts I discovered Townsend's instrument and solved its secret. You are a dolt, a stupid bungler! I need no such aides."

"But I told you Morris held the Secret—"

"Bah! There is no longer a secret to be held."

"But there is, Sire! Before he died, Morris told it to—"

Hardesty interrupted coldly, "Am I to understand, Garroway, that this man is no longer under your protection?"

Garroway shrugged.

"I have washed my hands of him," he said carelessly. "Come, guards!"

He turned away as Meacher screamed, vainly struggled to escape the vengeful trio closing in on him.

"Take him, Vurrth!" ordered Hardesty succinctly.

The great Venusian's hands closed briefly around the traitor's throat, stifling his garbled cries. With revealing ease he lifted the Earthman, held him dangling like a sack of meal in midair, and looked at Hardesty for orders.

"Put him down," commanded Neil. "We will settle our differences elsewhere."

Vurrth grunted, and obediently loosed his grip. The body, of Fred Meacher slumped to the floor awkwardly ... and lay still. Brian Shaughnessey bent over the crumpled figure. He glared up angrily at his comrade.

"Confound you, Vurrth! He's dead!"

Vurrth grinned slowly.

"Sor-ree," he said. "Maybe hold too tight?"

One of the guards, glancing back, muttered a word to his captain who, in turn, passed the message to the Overlord. A thin smile touched Garroway's lips, but he did not turn his head. The incident was, his attitude intimated as he led his entourage from the hall, a matter in which he took no concern whatsoever....

II

As at his captors' bidding he stepped into the great metal chamber which was the late Dr. Townsend's creation, two singular emotions filled Dirk Morris' mind. One of these was thankfulness, the second ... curiosity.

Fear was strangely absent. Perhaps that was because for many months Dirk and those with whom he conspired for the overthrow of Black Garroway's tyrannical rule had lived under a Damoclean sword. Death, long a silent guest at their every gathering, was a host whose imminence aroused no dread.

Dirk was thankful that he had been able to buy, with his own life, the freedom of his companions. Why the Emperor had been willing to strike this bargain, Dirk did not exactly understand; possibly because the Overlord held his enemies in contempt, now their leader was being removed; more likely because Garroway still held a lurking fear of those who plotted against him, and was freeing them only that his hireling spies might watch their movements.

But even that, thought Morris gratefully, was better than that all should die, and the Movement end. Hardesty now knew the Secret, and while one remained alive to work on that knowledge, hope endured.

The second commingling emotion, curiosity, concerned the chamber into which, at this very moment, he was stepping. A "disintegration chamber"

Garroway had called it, vowing his scientists had learned its method of operation. But in this, Dirk knew with positive assurance, the Overlord was mistaken. Utterly mistaken. Yet, if it were not a disintegration machine, then what—?

There was no time for further thought. The door was closed; through the thick pane Morris saw Garroway nod, saw a soldier close the switch on the instrument's control-board.

For an instant the thin hum of current filled Dirk's ears; a terrific impact of pure electrical energy pierced his every nerve and fiber with flaming hammers of agony. He felt his knees buckle beneath him, was vainly aware that his mouth opened to cry aloud noiselessly.

A strange, twisting vibration wrenched and tore him; the solid walls about him seemed to melt and writhe at angles the eyes ached to follow. All this he saw as in the throes of wild delirium. Then, unable to longer bear the fearful pain, every sinew of his being tensed for an intolerable instant ... then darkness, blessed darkness, rushed in to claim Dirk Morris. He sank, weak and senseless, into its enfolding arms.

*

Silence.

Silence and darkness.

Then, out of the silence, sound. Out of the infinite darkness, light. Light, and warmth, and comfort.

Dirk Morris opened his eyes.

He opened his eyes ... then closed them again, shaking his head to rid his fancy of its weird hallucination. Beside him a voice spoke soft, rippling syllables that held no meaning. Another voice replied; a masculine voice, equally soft, but elderly and grave.

The possessor of the first voice, pressed a cup to Morris' lips. An unknown liquor tingled Dirk's palate and swept the lethargy from his veins. He stirred and lifted himself to one elbow, stared about him incredulously.

"Where—?" he began—"where on earth—?" Then he stopped, seeing the sky above him, the ground supporting him, those who were his Samaritans. A poignant regret seized him. He whispered, "*Not* on Earth. Then the ancient religions were true? There *is* an afterlife ... a Heaven peopled with angels."

The girl kneeling beside him laughed, her voice like the music of rill waters. She turned to her elder companion, said in strange, accented English, "See, I was right, father! He *is* from over There. I recognized the garments; severe and ugly. Not at all like *ours*—"

She touched the flowing hem of her own brief, silken kirtle with fingers equally soft and white. Both she and the graybeard were dressed in clothing of classic simplicity. No stiff military harness like that worn by earthlings of Dirk's era, but something resembling the *chiton* of ancient Greece.

Dirk said wonderingly, "You ... you're human!"

"But, of course, stranger."

"This ... this isn't Earth, though. Nor any planet of the System!"

Dirk gestured toward the landscape, smooth and gaily gardened, stretching from horizon to horizon with no ornament save the natural adornments of Nature. Here were no grim and ugly buildings towering to the skies, blocking the sun's warm rays from view; no shining mansions flanked by filthy hovels; none of the cheek-and-jowl splendor and squalor of the world whence he had come. Here was only gentle, untrammeled beauty in a quiet, pastoral existence.

No planet of the Solar System was so organized, Dirk knew. But were a second, convincing proof needed, he had but to glance at the sky. There shone not the lone, familiar Sun of Earth ... but *two* suns! A binary system. One golden-yellow like Sol, the other a bluish-white globe of radiance.

"No," answered the elderly man, "this is neither the Earth from which you came nor any planet of its system. This is the planet Nadron, satellite of the twin suns, Kraagol and Thuumion, in the fourth galactic level."

Triumph was a bursting bomb in Morris' heart.

"Then it was a success, after all!" he cried. "Then Townsend was right! If only he had lived to see this day! A success ... and all because Garroway's scientists, playing with an instrument they did not understand, succeeded where we had failed for years!

"But ... but your planet is unfamiliar to me; I do not know your suns by the names you have given them. Your system lies just where in relation to the galactic center? How many miles ... or light years ... are we from my native Earth?"

The old man looked at him oddly for a moment, then:

"We are *no* miles from your Earth, my friend," he announced quietly, "and the distance may be measured in *seconds* ... not light-years."

Dirk stared, bewilderment in his eyes.

"I ... I'm afraid I don't understand, sir. I hope you will forgive me. Perhaps you are joking—?"

"It is no jest, my boy, but the simple truth. Earth and Nadron are ... but, stay! Let me prove my point otherwise. Has it not occurred to you to wonder that we, the people of a foreign world, know your language?"

Dirk said wonderingly, "Why ... why, that's right; you do! But how—?"

"Because," explained the elder, "we have listened to it being spoken for many, many years. Over our visors we have both heard and watched you on your neighboring world."

"Neighboring world?"

"How came you here?" asked the old man. "What means of propulsion brought you hither?"

That, at least, Dirk knew. He answered eagerly.

"I came here through the medium of the greatest discovery ever made by man. The *teleport*, a machine invented by Robert Townsend. A perfect solution to the long puzzling problem of material transport through Space. It disassembles the atoms of any body placed in its transmitting chamber, and reconstructs that body at a destination selected by a setting of its dials.

"Through circumstances not of my own choosing, I was a subject of that machine. I was forced into the transmitter by ... well, it does not matter whom ... and my body broadcast to this spot. Though I do not yet, sir, understand just where I am, or exactly how I reached here—"

The old man shook his head regretfully.

PHANTOM OUT OF TIME

"I am sorry, my boy, to tell you the machine did not work as was planned. Its theory was sound; in one respect it performed as expected. It *did* disassemble your atomic components, did reconstruct your body elsewhere. But it was to no far bourne your journey carried you.

"*Your body still stands in exactly the spot it stood before the machine operated!*"

*

For a long, uncomprehending moment Dirk Morris gaped at his informant. At last his bedazement found words.

"Oh, now, surely you can't expect me to believe—"

"No," interrupted the graybeard gently, "not without visual evidence. Rima, my dear—?"

He turned to the girl, who nodded and from the folds of her garment produced a shimmering crystal object; a mirror of some sort, or a lens. This she handed to Dirk.

"If you will look through this—?" she suggested.

Morris lifted the crystal to his eyes wonderingly ... then almost dropped it in his excitement!

Beneath his feet still lay the lush greensward of an alien world, but through the curious crystal he gazed upon no panorama of soft, rolling hills and pleasant valleys. Before him lay the image of a scene he had but recently quitted: the execution dock of Graed Garroway's prison!

A few feet to his right stood the metal chamber into which he had been thrust, the supposed "disintegration cell." Through the viewpane of this the Overlord was peering, a grim smirk of satisfaction on his lips. As Dirk watched, Garroway turned and gestured to the guardsman whose hand had depressed the activating switch. Dirk heard no words, but could easily read the movement of the Emperor's lips.

"*Enough! It is done!*"

With an instinct born of illogic, Dirk reached forth as if to grip the throat of the murderous Garroway. In doing so, the crystal left his eyes. Instantly the scene vanished. He looked once more upon distance-purpled hills softly limned in the splendor of two suns.

14

The girl laughed softly.

"Confusing at first, isn't it? But you'll soon—"

"Please!" begged Dirk hoarsely. "I must see—" He placed the mirrorlike object once more to his eyes, saw Graed Garroway lead the way from the execution chamber. Awkwardly, uncertainly, Morris took a step forward ... another. Though he knew his feet trod the soil of the planet Nadron, to his eyes it seemed he glided forward across the floor of the prison.

The door swung to behind Garroway and his followers, and involuntarily Dirk flinched ... then grunted reproof at his own needless gesture. So far as he was concerned, that heavy metal barrier did not exist. For the briefest fraction of an instant his vision was blotted by jet darkness, then he stood outside the door, looking down the corridor.

He hastened forward, stumbling, as feet that appeared to be traversing smooth floors actually trod uneven soil, and paused at last, an invisible presence at the tableau next enacted. He witnessed his friends' release from the cell, read the movement of Hardesty's dry lips as Neil whispered, "*It ... it is over?*" He saw Garroway's boastful warning, Brian's hot denial, then watched—first with dazed incomprehension, then with fierce understanding—the betrayal, panic and execution of Fred Meacher.

*

When Meacher's corpse lay on the floor at ... or so it seemed ... his very feet, and the comrades left the hallway, he would again have followed them. But at that moment he landed with a solid bump against something hard, and with a start he looked from the crystal to find a tree before him. More than a hundred yards away waited those who had befriended him. He retraced his steps slowly to their company.

"Now you understand and believe, my boy?" the kindly alien asked.

"I believe," said Dirk simply. "But, sir—"

"My name, man of Earth, is Slador. On this world, I am known as the Ptan Slador, which is to say 'teacher.' This is my daughter, Rima."

"I am called Morris. Dirk Morris. I also—" Dirk spoke bitterly—"have a number, as have all Earthmen of this unhappy century. Yes, Ptan Slador, I believe, but even yet I do not understand. I stand in one world, but looking through your crystal I see into another: my own. Why is this?"

"Because, Dirk Morris, our two worlds lie adjacent."

"Adjacent? You mean in Space?"

"I mean in Space-Time. Look, my young friend ... your Earth science knows of the atom?"

"But of course. It is the building-block of matter. The smallest indivisible unit—"

"Exactly. Yet even this minute fleck of matter, the building-block of worlds, so small that it cannot be observed under man's strongest microscopes, is composed of ninety-nine per cent *empty space*!

"Or, let me say, rather ... what *appears* to be such to the men of all universes. Actually, there is no emptiness in the atom. It is composed of solid matter, but the individual zerons of this single entity are all vibrating at a different frequency in the Greater Universe which includes *all* of Space and Time.

"Consequently, you on Earth, existing at one rate of vibration, see an entire universe vibrating at a period which matches your own. We of Nadron live under another vibration. Our solidity, our world, our universe ... these are all part of the 'emptiness' of *your* world, just as *your* existence forms a part of the emptiness of *our* atom. Do you see?"

"Vaguely," said Dirk humbly. "Only vaguely. We, the young men of my era, are not an educated people, Ptan Slador. There was a time in Earth's history when all men were free to study where and as they wished, read what they willed. It is not so now. Only the highborn are permitted to own books, or borrow them from the Overlord's crypts; only those designated by the Emperor are taught to read and write. The rest of us, hungry for a crust of knowledge, must gather in hidden places to learn our letters from instructors who risk their lives to teach us."

"You mean," cried the girl, "one man has dared grasp so much power? So much evil power?"

Slador nodded gravely.

"Yes, my dear. I have long believed some such situation existed on our neighbor world. From scenes I have witnessed through the visor, snatches of whispered conversation, I guessed such might be the case. It is a sorry plight for a once proud world. Drowned in a sea of ignorance, sunken in a slough of misery and despair, mankind is beaten helpless—"

Dirk laughed gratingly.

"Pardon me, sir. Not beaten. Not helpless. We are ignorant, yes ... but not yet have all of us abandoned hope of striking off our shackles.

"We have a secret organization, fostered by the late Dr. Townsend, led until recently by myself, now headed by the bravest of my former comrades: Neil Hardesty. The members of this clan are pledged to one purpose ... the overthrow of Graed Garroway, tyrant of the Solar System.

"Our greatest hope for success lay in Dr. Townsend's invention, the *teleport*. It is quite impossible to muster an armed band on any of the planets under Garroway's thumb. His spies are everywhere. Even—" Dirk finished bitterly—"among our own supposed comrades.

"Therefore we had planned to transport our bodies to some extra-Solar world, there gird ourselves for a last fight against Garroway's minions. That was our dream. But now—"

He paused, shaking his head sorrowfully. That dream was now ended. Dr. Townsend's secret weapon was not what had been hoped. Instead—

*

Then, even as he despaired, understanding drove home with blinding force. The weapon was *not* a failure! It was a success ... but in another way than had been planned. He cried aloud: "But, yes! I've been blind! This way is just as good ... perhaps better!"

"What way, Dirk Morris?" asked the girl.

"There is no need to seek a far planet of a far sun! We planned that solely because we did not know anything about the existence of your world, your universe.

"Nadron shall be our rallying spot! It is the ideal spot wherein to gather our forces. Close to Earth ... seconds, not light-years, from the foe we would crush—"

"A moment, Earthman!" interrupted Slador. "You mean to use our world as the breeding-place for conflict on yours? Is that your thought?"

"But of course. What better place?"

The Ptan shook his head gravely.

"I am sorry, my son. But I fear that is impossible. The Council would never permit it."

"Council?"

"Our government. Here we have a World Council, made up of the oldest and wisest amongst us. Many, many centuries ago the question was raised as to whether we of Nadron should establish and maintain intercourse between our neighboring planets.

"After a lengthy period of observation and study, it was decided we should not. It was the Council's judgment—" Here Slador flushed with thin apology—"that Earth is in too primitive a stage of development for such a union.

"Wherever and whenever we watched affairs unfolding, we saw war, strife, bickering and discontent. We saw poverty and hunger ... perils unknown in our own quiet civilization. We heard the roar of gunfire and the bombastic mouthings of warlords. We found, in short, no culture worthy of inclusion in our own placid existence.

"At that time was the Law laid down ... that we of Nadron should not embroil ourselves in Earth's affairs until such time as a civilized Earth should be able to meet us on a plane of equal amity.

"Therefore—" sighed the Ptan—"despite my private sympathy with your cause, I am compelled to warn you that you may not use Nadron as host for your gathering forces. Though a peaceful world, we have means of enforcing this edict. I am sorry, but you must develop other plans."

Dirk stared at the speaker strickenly, realizing the logic of all Slador had said, but feeling, nevertheless, sick despair that Earth's past madnesses should now so destroy the only chance of present salvation. He turned to the girl, who returned his gaze with a helpless little shrug of sympathy.

He wet his lips, said hoarsely, "But ... but if you do not help us, Earth is doomed to tyranny for countless decades to come. You cannot refuse us your aid—"

Slador said smoothly, surprisingly, "I have not said I would not aid you. I have merely forbidden your forces the soil of Nadron. But there are ... other ways of helping. Ways not under the ban of our Council's sage decision."

Hope surged in Morris like a welling tide.

"There are?" he cried. "What ways, Ptan Slador?"

"Have you forgotten," asked Slador, "the strangeness of your own existence here? Or is it that you do not yet see how this can be bent to use? Listen, my son—"

He spoke, and Dirk Morris listened with ever growing interest.

III

Corporal Ned Tandred, Precinct Collector of Taxes in the Ninth Ward, Thirty-Fourth district of Greater Globe City, did not like his job.

As he wheeled his unicar through the twilight shaded streets of the city, hemmed by a rush of bustling traffic, he thought regretfully of those from whom he had this day forced payment of tithes—tribute—they could ill afford.

An old man ... an even older widow ... the husband of an invalid wife and father of three small children ... a young man unable, now new taxes had been exacted, to marry the girl who had been waiting for him seven long years ... these were just a few of the humble lives the Emperor's recent edict had driven to newer, deeper, sloughs of despair. And he, Corporal Tandred, had been the unwilling instrument through which Garroway had dipped once again into the pockets of his subjects.

"Subjects!" grunted Corporal Tandred. "Not subjects ... slaves! That's what we are, all of us. Myself included!" He tugged savagely at the handle of his unicar, careening the tiny one-wheeled vehicle perilously to the curb of the avenue as a gigantic, gray-green armored tanker of the Imperial Army roared belligerently up the center of the street, hogging the road and scattering traffic before it. "Miserable serfs, all of us! If I thought there were half a chance of getting away with it, I'd skip this filthy uniform and—"

He stopped suddenly, a strange sensation coming over him. The sensation of somehow being watched ... listened to.

He peered cautiously over his shoulder. No ... no one in the car but himself. The communications unit was dull; no chance his rebellious grumbling had been overhead by a keen-eared Headquarters clerk.

Corporal Tandred breathed a sigh of relief. Nerves. Just plain nerves ... that was all that bothered him. That was the result of living under constant surveillance, inescapable oppression. You got the feeling of never being free.

"This cursed money!" he grumbled again. "If I could get away with it, I'd throw it in the Captain's face! In the Overlord's face! Thieving—"

Once more he stopped in midsentence, his lips a wide and fearful O of bewilderment. This time he had made no mistake! There *was* someone near him. A voice spoke in his ear.

"*Make no such foolish gesture, Corporal!*"

Corporal Tandred recovered control of his car with a sudden effort. He depressed its decelerating button, drew it to the curb, and stared wildly about him.

"W-who said that?" he demanded hoarsely. "Where are you?"

"*Who speaks,*" said the quiet, insistent voice, "*does not matter. Nor the spot from whence I speak. The important thing is that you hear and obey my words. Make not the error of hurling the tribute money in anyone's face. Deliver it to your superior officer—but see that you get a signed receipt for it. Do you understand?*"

"No!" said Corporal Tandred weakly. "I hear a voice speaking, but see no one. I don't understand—"

"*It is not necessary that you understand. Just obey. Get a signed receipt for that money. That is all!*"

"Wait!" cried Corporal Tandred. "Wait a minute—!" He was talking to himself. Even as he spoke, he sensed that. The strange, semi-electrical feeling of a nearby presence was gone.

*

For a moment he sat stock-still, trying to sooth his ruffled nerves. His effort was not altogether successful; he started the unicar with a jerk, and sped down the avenue at a rate of speed forbidden by civic ordinance. A uniformed attendant frowned disapproval as he screeled to a stop in front of the Revenue Office, but Corporal Tandred paid him no heed. He hurried straightway to the central office, there deposited his collections before his captain.

The captain nodded abstractedly, then, his attention drawn by some oddness in the subaltern's appearance, raised a questioning eyebrow.

"What is it, Tandred? Anything wrong?"

"N-no, sir," said the corporal uncertainly.

"Someone make a complaint? That it?"

"Well, sir, there *were* several complaints. Citizens find these new taxes hard to swallow, sir; very hard."

The captain laughed derisively.

"Sheep! Let them suffer. It is no concern of ours. The Overlord has a militia to maintain. Well ... that is all."

He waved a hand in dismissal. Corporal Tandred said hesitantly, "Yes, sir. But the ... the receipt, sir?"

"Receipt? For what?"

"For the money, sir. Regulations, sir."

"Oh, yes." The captain grinned caustically. "Don't you trust me, Corporal? You never asked for a receipt before that I can remember."

"N-no, sir. I mean ... of course I trust you, sir. I just thought that ... that this being a new tax—"

"Very well; very well!" The captain scribbled, tore a receipt from his pad, and handed it to the underling. "You may go now, Corporal."

"Yes, sir. Thank you, sir."

Corporal Tandred left hurriedly, still uncertain *why* he had obeyed the instructions of the mysterious voice, still uncomprehending as to *why* he should have asked for a receipt, but with a strong conviction he had done the wise thing.

PHANTOM OUT OF TIME

He was right! Five minutes later the money vanished mysteriously from the captain's desk. Or so, at any rate, in stern, judicial court the captain swore repeatedly to an even colder superior. In vain the captain protested his innocence and tried to shift the blame to Corporal Tandred's shoulders. The Corporal was in the clear, triumphantly acquitted through possession of a signed receipt for the missing money.

In the bleak gray of the following dawn, the captain was shot for theft and conspiracy against the State. But the money was not found among his effects....

*

Brian Shaughnessey, crouched in the concealment of a flowering hedge, heard the footsteps of the guard pass within scant inches of his head. He counted slowly to himself.

"... eight ... nine ... ten...."

Noiselessly he gathered himself for the silent dash. Watchful waiting had taught him that ten seconds after marching past this bush, the guard turned briefly down a side lane from which the roadway was invisible. A hurried run, a swift and silent dash, would take him to the doorway of the supply warehouse.

He crouched, tensed, listened ... then ran. For a big man he made little noise. He had reached his objective with seconds to spare before the guard, returning from the bypath, glanced up and down the main avenue, found all clear, and resumed his rounds.

Shaughnessey grinned, slipped into the shadow of the doorway, and fumbled at his belt. He withdrew a metal ovoid, prepared to draw the pin that set its mechanism into operation ... then stopped! His fingers faltered, and he whirled, eyes darting anxiously. For from the darkness, a voice had spoken.

"No, Brian!"

Brian Shaughnessey shook himself like a great, shaggy dog. He was a strong man, a man of great courage. But he was also a superstitious man. Awe dawned now in his eyes. "This is it, then," he whispered to himself. "I'm not long for this world. It ... it's *him*, come to meet me. Well—" He shrugged—"if that's the way it must be, I might as well finish this job—"

And again he reached for the pin. But this time the sense of unseen presence was so strong that Brian Shaughnessey could almost feel the grip of ghostly fingers tingling on his wrist. And the voice was louder, clearer.

"*No, Brian! Not here!*"

"Morris!" cried Shaughnessey starkly, unbelievingly. "Dirk Morris!"

"*Hush, you idiot!*" warned the voice. "*You'll bring the guard down upon us!*"

"Us?" repeated Brian, baffled.

"*Don't toss that grenade here. You're too close to the munitions bins. Here ... let me have it!*"

Shaughnessey, stricken with a near-paralysis of awe, felt a curious vibration tingle through his fingers as from his slackened grip the explosive ovoid slipped ... and vanished! He stared about him wildly, gasped, "The grenade! Where did it go? Dirk—"

"*Not now!*" whispered the urgent voice. "*Go to Neil. Tell him to gather the Group at the regular place tonight. I will come to you. Now, get out of here. Quickly!*"

"B-but I don't understand—" gulped Brian.

"*Quickly!*" insisted the voice.

Shaughnessey nodded. He did not in the least understand what manner of mystery here confronted him. But he was a faithful servant of the Group. It was enough for him that he had heard Dirk Morris' voice, and that voice issued orders. Without another word he turned and slipped across the pathway to the cover of the hedge. Using it as a shelter, he fled the vicinity of the warehouse.

It was well he did so. Less than two minutes later, a terrific blast hurled him headlong to the ground as a bolt of man-made lightning seared the munitions dump wherein was stored the bulk of Graed Garroway's military supplies for this area. A livid stalk of greasy smoke, flame-laced, mushroomed to the skies, and the terrain for miles around was shaken as by a temblor.

When the ensuing fire was finally brought under control, there remained but charred and twisted girders in that gaping pit which once had been a

PHANTOM OUT OF TIME

fortress....

*

Lenore Garroway hummed softly to herself as she sat before the gorgeous, full-length mirror of her dressing-room table. She was happy ... and that was not altogether commonplace, because for an Emperor's daughter, surrounded by ease and every comfort, dwelling in the lap of luxuries few others even dared dream of, Lenore Garroway was not often happy.

But she was now, because she was with her gems. No pleasure in the seven worlds compared, in the Princess Lenore's mind, with that of fondling her precious stones, rare and perfect specimens gathered from the farflung corners of the System at the cost of no one dared guess how many lives.

Before and about her in bounteous array lay a ransom of glittering baubles. Chalcedony and sardonyx ... diamond and ruby ... the rare green *pharonys* delved from the sea-bottoms of Venus, the even rarer ice-amethyst of Uranus ... *wisstrix* from giant Jupiter and the faceted *koleidon* of tiny Eros ... these were her playthings.

So she sat, allowing the glittering motes to sift through her soft, white fingers, raising this matched set of rings to her ears, that exquisite lavaliere to her equally exquisite throat, humming softly to herself as she sat at her dressing table, watching the graceful movements of her perfect body in the full-length rock-quartz mirror.

A soft tap pulsed through the room, and the Princess Lenore turned, the flicker of a frown marring the perfection of her brow.

"Well, Marta?" she demanded.

Her maid-in-waiting entered fearfully. She was old and ugly. The Princess would not have about her any who were not; her radiance must be at all times like that of a true jewel amidst paste. Even the ladies of the court were required to dress down their own lesser beauty when gathered for state occasions.

"Well, Marta?" repeated the princess.

"Your pardon, Highness," breathed the old woman. "A delegation from the women of the city—"

"What do they want?"

"It is something about ... taxes, Highness. They say they cannot afford—"

"Taxes!" The princess' eyes clouded. "Why must they fret me with their miserable woes? I know nothing of taxes. Bid them see my father."

Marta cringed humbly.

"They have tried to, Highness, but without success. That is why they have come here. To beg your intercession—"

"I cannot see them," said Lenore. "Tell them to go away. I am busy."

"But, Highness—"

"Away, I said!" The princess' voice was silken-soft no longer; it flamed with sudden petulance. "I am too busy to hear their petty grievances. Send them away! And you, too!"

With abrupt, feline violence she snatched a handful of baubles from the table before her, hurled them at the aged servant. Marta stood like a withered Danae beneath the rich rain, whined, "Yes, Highness," and disappeared. The princess shut intrusion from her mind as the door closed. She turned once more to her playthings, picked up and fondled a pendant of intricately interwoven sapphire and *tolumnis*. Its green-and-scarlet flame burned cold against the smooth satin of her breast. She hummed softly to herself, happy....

It was then the voice spoke.

The voice was a man's voice. Its masculine deepness was like the rasp of grating steel in the languid femininity of this room.

"*Send them away, eh, Princess? Very well. As you have judged, so shall it also be judged against you!*"

The Princess Lenore whirled to the doorway, startled white hands leaping to her throat. Her gray-green eyes were wide with shock ... and horror. They widened even more as they found ... no one!

"Wh-where are you?" she gasped. "Who dares enter the boudoir of the Princess Lenore?"

She heard no sound of footsteps, but the voice drew nearer with each word.

"*I so dare, Princess.*"

"And ... and who are you?"

"*My name does not matter. But you may call me Conscience, if you must give me a name. For I am the Conscience of an empire.*"

The voice was beside Lenore now. She spun swiftly, her hands seeking emptiness about her.

"It is a trick! Someone will die for this! Leave! Leave this instant, or I call the guard—"

The voice of "Conscience" laughed.

"*Call the guard if you will, Princess. I will have gone ere they arrive ... and these with me!*"

This time the sound came from *behind* her. Again the girl whirled, this time to see a stupefying sight. As if imbued with eerie lapidary life, the jewels were rising from her dressing-table in great handfuls. Leaping clots of rich iridescence climbed into thin air ... and vanished!

*

Up till now the princess had been overwhelmed with shock; now she was struck to the quick with another emotion. She screamed aloud and darted forward in defense of her precious gems.

"Stop! They are mine! How dare you—?"

Her questing hands touched the disappearing jewels, and for an instant a strange, electrical tingling coursed her veins. Then the warmth of a human hand struck down her clawing fingers; the Voice cried sternly, "*Let be, woman! These go to those who need them more than you!*" Then with a quick change of tone, "*Stand still, you little hell-cat—*"

The Princess Lenore had flung herself forward upon the invisible thief, was groping with maddened fingers at a face, at eyes she could not see. Her hands touched flesh ... her ears caught the swift sibilance of an indrawn breath. In all her life, never had Lenore been in such close contact with a man. Strong arms gripped her shoulders, shook her fiercely, an angry voice grated, "*You greedy little fool! Are these all you live for, then? Cold stones? No wonder your heart is an icy barren, without sympathy or compassion. Don't you know what it means to hunger and be without bread, to want and be without hope, to love and be without love? In all your life, have you known only the icy caress of gems? Not this—?"*

And harshly, stunningly, the cries of the Princess Lenore were stifled by the crush of male lips upon her own. For an instant the world spun dizzily beneath her; it seemed a burning brand raced through her veins, crying a tocsin. A vast, engulfing weakness shook the princess; she fell back, trembling and shaken.

Then anger, fierce and bitter, cleared her senses. She opened her eyes ... and found herself viewing an incredible sight: herself bent to the embrace of a tall, dark-haired man clad in the rough habiliments of the working class. A young man whose jacket pockets bulged with the jewels that had disappeared ... a young man whose eyes were covered with a pair of strangely shaped spectacles....

With a start, she realized she was seeing her formerly invisible guest in the rock-quartz mirror. At her gasp, the stranger spun, saw his reflection in the glass. With an oath he loosed her, seized a heavy stool, and hurled it at the glass. Its smoothness shattered into a thousand gleaming splinters ... and once again she saw no one.

"*Vixen!*" grated the voice. For a few more seconds, jewels continued to leap upward into what the Princess Lenore now knew were hidden pockets, while she stood helplessly by. Then—she never could explain just *why*, but by some curious *absence* of sensation she knew—the boudoir was deserted save for herself.

The Princess Lenore stared long and wonderingly at what had been a mirror, the most perfect example of Plutonian rock-quartz crystal ever moulded. Then one soft hand lifted strangely to lips which still tingled ... and something like a smile, a thoughtful smile, touched those lips.

Then, at long last, the Princess Lenore called the guard.

IV

Neil Hardesty peered anxiously at the chronometer on his wrist. He said, "Almost midnight. Brian, are you sure it was—?"

"Positive!" said Brian Shaughnessey stubbornly. "It was Dirk Morris, Neil. You've got to believe me. I know how it sounds. Crazy. But it was him."

"You didn't *see* him," reminded Hardesty gently. "You were under great stress. It might have been an hallucination, you know."

"Was that explosion," demanded Shaughnessey, "imagination? It blew the warehouse plumb from here to Tophet. If I'd been within five hundred yards, I'd have been blown to a bunch of rags. It was him, Neil. I'd know his voice any time, any place."

Vurrth said thoughtfully, "But Dirk dead, no?"

"That's what we *thought*," said Brian doggedly. "But he ain't dead. Either he's still alive, or his ghost—" A strange look swept his features. He stopped, glanced at the new leader of the group. "Neil, could it have been a—"

"I don't know," confessed Hardesty. "I honestly do not know. We'll just have to wait and see, Brian. But if he's coming here tonight, he'd better come soon. It's almost midnight. After the curfew, we won't be allowed to move on the streets."

"Particularly," interjected a new member of the Group, "now. The Overlord's guards are watching the streets like a pack of hounds since the theft of the Princess' jewels."

Hardesty said staunchly, "They can't blame that on us. We were all at work when it happened. Still ... I'd like to know who did it. I'd like to know what became of them, too. Disappeared into thin air, the Princess claimed—"

"*The jewels,*" said a familiar voice, "*have been distributed where they will do the most good. Their wealth has been converted into food to fill the bellies of those who hunger.*"

All occupants of the refuge spun as one, seeking in vain the speaker. Neil Hardesty cried:

"Dirk! Then Brian was right! But ... where are you?"

The voice from nowhere chuckled.

"That is what Garroway would like to know. I am beside you, Neil. Reach out your hand."

Hardesty did so. Briefly he felt a strange, warm tingling ... then his hand met and gripped the hand of Morris. Tears sprang to the Group leader's eyes. He choked, "Dirk! Thank the gods you have returned! We thought you were—"

He hesitated over the word. Morris supplied it.

"Dead? I am, Neil ... so far as you are concerned."

All members of the listening party stirred uneasily. Vurrth grunted, and Brian Shaughnessey husked, "You see? I guessed it. A ghost—"

"That's right," laughed Morris in most unwraithlike tones. "A ghost. A galactic ghost ... free to roam the System without hindrance or bar. Fleshless at will ... but with a body if I so desire."

"You ... you mean," choked Neil, "you can make yourself visible if you wish?"

"Not visible to your eyes, no. But I can render myself solid when it is necessary to do so. It was thus—" Morris laughed—"I stole the tax-collector's gleanings and the Princess Lenore's jewels. Thus, too, I helped Brian destroy the munitions dump."

"I'm afraid," said Hardesty humbly, "I'm afraid I do not understand, Dirk. You are fleshless ... yet you can make your body solid. You are alive, yet you call yourself 'dead so far as we are concerned.' What does it mean?"

"I'm not sure," answered Morris, "that I understand it myself, completely. But here is the explanation as it was told me—"

*

He told them, then, of that which had followed his "execution" in the teleport. Of his meeting with Ptan Slador and Rima, and that which had transpired between them. To a group such as this, untutored and unlettered, it was vain to speak in technical language; he told his story as simply as possible.

"—thus," he concluded, "though the laws of Nadron forbid our using that adjacent world as a gathering-spot for our forces, the Ptan Slador and his fellows are sympathetic to our cause. They, therefore, instructed me in the use of their visor, as well as in the employment of certain strange faculties developed in me by my passage through the teleport.

PHANTOM OUT OF TIME

"I am, you see, no longer simply a man of Earth, but a creature of two worlds. Through the machination of the teleport, my atomic vibration was altered to that of Nadron's galactic universe. But in the greater continuum of Space-Time, there remains a life-path which is mine, and typically mine.

"To this ineradicable life-path I am always free to return. Could you see me, you would note that I wear two odd bits of apparel. One, a pair of visor-spectacles secured to my eyes; the second, a force-belt which enables me to give my invisible body substance when such is needed.

"To reach any given spot on Earth, I have but to go to its matching spot on Nadron, then turn the stud upon the force-belt. This sends a magnetic flux through my body, diverting it from Nadron's vibration to that of Earth ... and placing me on my home planet. But as for visibility—" He shook his head sadly—"that I can never be again ... to you. There are limits to the diversion of matter. My only *real* existence now is upon Nadron; my visits to Earth can be made only as a tangible and vengeful wraith."

"Then we can never see you again, Dirk?"

"Not on Earth. On Nadron, perhaps. The Ptan Slador has promised that when we have rid Earth of its tyrant, intercourse may be opened between our two worlds. Not before, though." Dirk pondered briefly. "There is one other way," he said. "A way which I did not know of myself until a few hours ago. But I shall not mention it, even to you. It was an accident which happened in the Princess' boudoir. I must ask the Ptan about it when next I see him. Meanwhile—"

"Yes?" said Brian eagerly. "What do we do, Dirk?"

"You," ordered Morris sternly, "get out of sight and lay low! All of you! The incidents which have occurred today are but a mild beginning to what is to come. There is about to burst loose a reign of terror such as Graed Garroway in the depth of his infamy never dreamed possible ... and I am its originator!

"When this begins, Garroway's first logical move will be to herd all known living members of the Group together for questioning. You know the manner of his interrogation. You must be spared the pleasures of his rack and brand.

30

"So ... hide! Go where you can, as swiftly as you can, and forget you have heard from me. But spread the word to all freedom-loving men that the time approaches when Earth and the solar system will rid itself of Garroway's shackles. You can do this from concealment?"

"We can," said Hardesty eagerly. "We can and will, Dirk. The hearts of millions are with us. If you will but tell us when and where to strike."

"You will be told from time to time. When word does not come, you will know to strike where a weakness has been driven in the enemy's defenses."

The voice of Dirk Morris was not pleasant now. It rang with the bitter hardness of forged steel.

"I will strike Garroway hard, and often, and everywhere! Where least he expects attack, there will I strike him. His armies will be robbed of leaders, stores, strongholds. I will make Earth a boiling hell for him. And when Earth becomes too hot a cauldron for his tasting, to the far planets of the System I will pursue him inexorably. This I vow by the bond of comradeship we have pledged!"

Hardesty asked, "Far planets, Dirk? You can leave Nadron, then?"

"Yes. There is no time for further explanation now, though. You must get into hiding immediately. For tonight begins the vengeance we have so long waited. Until happier days, then, my friends—"

The voice dimmed with the final words. An electric tenseness left the air, and somehow the assembled listeners knew their visitor had gone. Neil Hardesty shook himself.

"Goodbye, Dirk, and ... good luck!"

Then, to his companions, "Well ... that's all. Now we know what to expect. Come on ... let's get going! There's a lot of work ahead of us, as well as Morris."

*

Already back on the fair soil of Nadron, Dirk Morris had retraced his wanderings to the home of the Ptan Slador. He approached its "doorway," marveling again—as he had when first the Ptan revealed the entrance to his domicile—at the ease with which the portal merged itself into the surrounding landscape.

Homes on Nadron, Dirk had learned, were *underground!* That was why the eye beheld nothing but the beauties of nature when the horizon was scanned. The functions of living were carried on in cleverly constructed subterranean dwelling-places, leaving the entire surface of the planet a playground for the pastoral race.

The Ptan was awaiting his return, eager curiosity in his eyes. He looked up as Morris entered.

"Well, my friend?" he asked.

Dirk smiled grimly.

"Very!" he replied. "It has been a day Graed Garroway will long remember ... if I give him a chance to do so."

"Your plans were successful?"

"Perfectly. I assisted one of my erstwhile comrades in the destruction of a vital munitions storehouse, robbed a tax collector of his monies and the Emperor's own daughter of her jewels, and distributed these where they were needed most ... amongst the poverty-ridden families of the capital." Morris chuckled. "There will be more surprised faces tomorrow when those poor devils wake to find themselves richer by a king's ransom than when they sought their pallets."

"Still," said Slador thoughtfully, "you have really accomplished little. It would take a thousand men as many years to redistribute the tribute Garroway's army has exacted from the people of your homeland—"

"That is true. But this is only a beginning; a few, minor incidents created to strike fear and awe into Garroway's hirelings. Later, I will strike at more vital spots. And as for men ... there will be not thousands, but millions, to rally when Garroway's force begins to weaken."

Slador nodded.

"Yes, that I believe. It is the history of mankind. Ever there have been millions to arise when oppression grows unbearable."

A remembered question stirred in Dirk's mind; something which had vaguely puzzled him in his previous conversations with the Nadronian. He asked, "How is it, Ptan Slador, you know so much about the history of Earthmen? And how, even more strangely, does it come about that you of Nadron and we of Earth are identical in physical structure? Man's space-vessels have flamed to the farthermost planets of our sun, but nowhere else was ever found a life-form similar to that on our own Earth.

"The Venusians resemble us, but are taller by many feet, heavier, slower of wit. The Plutonians again look like us ... save for the fact that their skins are green. Yet you, not only removed from our Solar Galaxy, but from our very ken of knowledge, might be a brother of my own."

The Ptan smiled slowly.

"And so, in fact, I am, Dirk Morris."

"What?"

"A brother many times and many centuries removed. Tell me ... have you never heard of the land of Aztlan?"

"Azt—?" Dirk pondered, shook his head. "No. I'm afraid I have not, Slador. Where was it ... or is it?"

"It was," answered the older man, "an island in the ocean you Earthmen now call the 'Atlantic' The very ocean takes its name from our once-great nation—"

"Aztlan!" ejaculated Morris. "Atlantis! Of course! Now I remember. It is a myth ... a fable ... of an island which sank beneath the waves countless centuries ago! But surely, sir, you don't mean—?"

*

"I mean," Slador assured him gravely, "that legend is no fable, but veritable truth. Yes, my son, there *was* such an island ... and we of Nadron were once the rulers of that island, and of your world.

"Its ancientness is not measured in centuries, but in millennia. How long we descendants of the Atlanteans have lived on Nadron, our archives do not tell. Those who fled hither from the holocaust that deluged our former home could not bring with them the impedimenta of a cultured civilization. We had to fight our way upward from semi-barbarism to our present state of living ... and even yet we have not regained all the lost lore of Aztlan."

Dirk said humbly, "Great must have been the wisdom of your forebears to be able to transfer themselves from a sinking island to this place. I understand, now, your interest in Earth. It is more than just sympathy for us ... it is a natural love for a land which once was yours."

"Yes," said the Ptan. "A land which once we ruled, and now have lost forever. But enough of this, my son. You were telling me of your adventures—?"

"Yes," said Dirk, remembering. "There was one thing happened which I do not understand. In the boudoir of the Princess Lenore, Ptan Slador, I was *visible* for a few seconds! Why was that?"

Slador stared at him in astonishment.

"Visible! Impossible!"

"That's what I thought. But it is true, sir. I saw my own image in the Princess' mirror—"

"Mirror! Ah!" exclaimed the Ptan. "Now I begin to understand. This mirror ... it was not plain, silvered glass? It was, perhaps, quartz?"

"Possibly," admitted Dirk. "I would not know about such things, sir."

"Undoubtedly," mused his advisor, "it *must* have been a rock-quartz mirror. That is the only Earthly substance of dual isotopic form. Its converse refractions hold and trap not only the normal vibrations of your system, but harmonic vibrations as well. Surely your scientists know this. Many hundreds of years ago, I know they experimented with the use of quartz substances in both light and sound transmission.

"But we are not so interested now in causes as in results. Do you think the Princess saw you in this mirror?"

"I ... I am afraid so," confessed Dirk. "It was her astonishment that attracted my gaze to the glass. Of course, I shattered the mirror instantly. But too late to keep her from seeing—"

"If, of course," interrupted a cool voice, "she was not as bemused as yourself."

"Eh?" Dirk spun, flushing in swift embarrassment as his eyes met those of

Slador's daughter. Rima's lips were lifted in a light smile which, oddly, was not altogether of amusement. "Oh, you mean ... then, you ... you saw?"

"You do let business interfere with pleasure, do you, Dirk Morris?" laughed the girl. "Yes, I am sorry, but I must confess to having been an innocent witness to your ... momentary digression. It was inexcusable of me, I know, but I was so interested in your endeavors that I turned on the visor to follow your adventures, and—"

"Rima," blurted Dirk, "you must believe me ... it was nothing. I mean, the Princess means nothing to me. I—"

He stopped, his embarrassment heightening with his color as he realized how any attempt at explanation merely made an already awkward situation worse. It suddenly mattered to him terribly that Rima should have watched that impulsive episode between himself and the Emperor's daughter. He had no right, he knew, to think of Rima as other than a girl who had befriended him on an alien world ... but somehow he already did. At first sight of her, a new meaning had entered into his life.

It did not soothe him that Rima turned away his explanation with a laughing shrug.

"Oh, but do not misunderstand me, Dirk Morris. It does not concern *me* in the least how you amuse yourself in your lighter moments. And your other exploits were, I must acknowledge, thrilling to watch ... in a somewhat different way."

Dirk said miserably, "Please! It was an impulse ... one I regretted immediately. The Princess Lenore means nothing to me ... nothing. I shall never lay eyes on her again in my life...."

V

In that one statement, Morris was mistaken. He made it in all good faith, but its truth was a matter over which he was not to have full control.

Two weeks passed. Two weeks filled with excitement and adventure. Two weeks during which Dirk Morris made good his pledge to the assembled brothers of the Group, now safely in hiding.

PHANTOM OUT OF TIME

During that fortnight the Galactic Ghost ... as soon he became known to the whispering citizenry of Earth ... struck again, again, and yet again at the wide-flung forces of Black Garroway. Some of these blows were of a minor nature: the theft of hoarded gold, and the subsequent reappearance, as if by magic, of that gold where starving folk could lay eager hands on it; the mysterious disappearance of the Emperor's armored unicar scant moments before Garroway was to make an impressive "personal appearance" before the populace of the capital city; the inexplicable vanishment of a secret formula wherewith the Overlord's military experts hoped to subdue the gallant little guerrilla army which still held a salient against Garroway's might on the planetoid Iris.

Other occurrences were more violent ... the kind that not even a ruthlessly controlled press can keep from public knowledge. The shocking demolition of the Overlord's strongest Asiatic fortress at Chuen-tzwan, keypoint from which his troops dominated all of what had once been Southern China. At six-fifteen in an evening, according to testimony given by the commanding officer at the subsequent investigation, from out of nowhere had appeared a placard, advising the entire garrison to withdraw immediately from the fortress, advising its component members, moreover, to rebel against Garroway. This ultimatum had teeth in it. Midnight was set as the deadline for obedience.

When at midnight the garrison was still abristle with an aroused and suspicious force of armed men, from a dozen key points had broken out instantaneous fires. "Only a member of the Imperial High Command," testified the wretched officer, "could have known where to set those fires. Each was at a vitally strategic place: near a munitions bin, a water supply depot, or a warehouse of inflammables. We were helpless. In an hour the entire fortress was doomed. I was lucky to save a tenth of my men."

He was not so fortunate in facing Garroway's wrath. The ex-commanding officer was put to death, along with every other ranking officer of the destroyed battalion.

This summary execution seemed bootless, though, when a day or so later

36

a similar flame destroyed the spaceport wherein was cradled one quarter of the Emperor's fleet. It was revealed by those who escaped this debacle that it had been impossible to salvage a single one of the spacecraft. "They were not merely attacked with fire from without," one official avowed. "Each vessel was found to have been tampered with by someone of the crew. The hypos were smashed as if with sledges, vital running parts were broken or stolen. We were helpless!"

Helpless ... helpless ... helpless! There were excuses Garroway heard often, far too often, during the next weeks. It was a word he learned to hate fiercely, because it was so true. In quick succession he saw fall his outpost in Lower Africa, the well-fortified city of Buenos Aires, the central armaments depot on Lake Huron. And each time the apologies were the same. "We saw no one ... heard no one ... until it was too late."

*

Meanwhile, trouble had reared its head challengingly in the capital city itself. Here, as elsewhere, a frightened populace began by asking, "Why?" and rapidly changed its query to the more daring, "Why not?"

Rumor, despite Garroway's every attempt to still it, ran like quicksilver through the city. If the press was silent on a new disaster, a common man or woman walking the streets might hear at his elbow a mysterious Voice asking, *"Did you know that last night the fortress at Toulon fell? The city is freed of the Emperor's rule; already the people have declared their independence, set up a provisional government. You can do the same. The hour is near!"*

Or a child, playing with his little companions on the streets, would suddenly stop and look about him strangely, listen as to an unseen speaker ... then run home to his parents with the inexplicable words of a Voice: *"Yesterday the Territory of Mexico threw off the Overlord's bonds. In a short while you may do the same. Prepare!"*

Or an unwimpled nun, praying in the sanctuary of a forbidden cloister—Black Garroway had long since outlawed the Church—might hear the vengeful, whispered tones of an unecclesiastic visitant: *"On Timor the*

Cross is worshipped openly since the Overlord's force has been broken. Here it will soon be the same. Spread the word!"

Thus the message was passed from person to person, and through a citizenry for decades apathetic to its own plight a new sense of hope and courage pulsed. Garroway's warriors sought in vain the refuge of the Group, upon the heads of whose members the Emperor had long since placed a tremendous price. But any common man who felt the urge to add his contribution to the rising tide of revolt could find that refuge with ease ... for at his work, or by his side, or in the heart of a crowd would be a Voice to tell him its location.

So grew revolt like a tropic vine, reaching out new tentacles with every rising dawn, developing new strength with every failure of Garroway's heretofore supposedly invulnerable war machine, gathering new converts with every fresh disaster. And the mute whisperings of fearful people began to thrum with a new and heady tone ... the spirit of daring, the renascense of the flame of liberty. The voice of the people ... which is the will of God.

Graed Garroway heard the bruitings of this voice, and was afraid.

*

Graed Garroway, whose boast had ever been he feared no man, heard the slow, insistent voice of revolt closing in about him ... and was afraid.

For the first time in his brutal career he had met an enemy he could not crush with ruthless blows, destroy by force, obliterate with a flick of the hand. His armies had fallen twice ... thrice ... a dozen times before a phantom, a will-o'-the-wisp that struck and fled, leaving terror, awe, and desolation in its wake.

He was baffled and confused, was Black Garroway. A terror was upon him that he could neither escape nor admit, for his confession of this fear to his commanders might be the last thing needed to send them, too, fleeing from his banner.

There was but one living soul to whom he dared admit this fear. That was his own flesh and blood, the Princess Lenore. Yet even to her he would not make an open avowal. His admission came in the form of blustering attack.

"Cowards!" he stormed, pacing the floor of his daughter's boudoir. "Snivelling cowards ... the lot of them! All this nonsense about a Voice ... a ghost that destroys strong forts ... a phantom that passes unscathed through flame ... *pah!* It's lies, lies ... nothing but lies!"

Princess Lenore studied her father lazily. She was not of the type easily stirred to fear. Under other circumstances, born the daughter of a lesser man than Black Garroway, Lenore Garroway might have made a name for herself in the world. As an adventuress ... a fighting-woman ... a daring woman.

She drawled, half amusedly, "Lies? Are you so sure of that, my father?"

"Sure?" snorted Graed Garroway. "Of course, I'm sure! There is no such thing as invisibility! My scientists have proven that time and time again in laboratories. The fabled 'magic cloak' of invisibility is both hypothetically and actually impossible. Where matter exists, there must be either reflection, refraction, or occultation—"

The Princess yawned.

"I do not understand these high-sounding words," she said, "nor need I. Because, you see, I have met the Galactic Ghost myself."

"Nonsense!" fumed her parent. "It was an hallucination you suffered. Sympathetic reaction set up by nervousness. The medical examiner testified—"

"Sometimes," interrupted the girl coldly, "you allow your ultrascientific viewpoint to warp your better judgment, my father. You talk nonsense! Could a nervous reaction account for the theft of my jewels, or the shattering of my mirror?"

"I am not denying," protested Black Garroway stiffly, "that the ... the Ghost visited you. Possibly he hypnotized you into believing him invisible. As for your broken mirror, that might have happened in a dozen ways—"

"The mirror was broken," said Lenore, "by the Ghost! Because I saw him reflected in it!"

"Furthermore, it is ridiculous to assume—" The Emperor stopped abruptly, his brow congealing—"Eh? What did you say? You saw—"

"I tried to tell you," purred the girl, "at the time. But you were too concerned with the loss of my gems to listen to me. I told you I saw the Galactic Ghost. He was a tall, dark-haired young man—"

"Ridiculous!" puffed Garroway. "More hypnosis!"

"—with crisp, curling hair," continued the Princess reminiscently, "and a small, triangular scar over his right eyebrow. A very interesting young man—"

*

Garroway had stiffened at her words, but this time it was with a tensing of interest. He leaned forward.

"A moment, my dear. Did you say ... a small scar above his right eyebrow?"

"Why, yes."

"A triangular scar? You are certain of that?"

"Positive. Why?"

"Because if you are right—" The Overlord left the sentence dangling; strode to the wall audio and crisped sharp orders into its metallic throat. Elsewhere in the palace a corps of underlings went into action, collecting swiftly the information demanded by their master. Within minutes there came a messenger, bearing a portfolio. This Garroway pawed through, selecting a photograph which he handed to the girl.

"Is this," he asked hoarsely, "the image you saw?"

The Princess Lenore took the photo, studied it, and nodded. "It is. I remember him well. Who is he?"

Graed Garroway laughed. But now there was a touch of hysteria in his laughter, and his deeprooted fear struck new depths as he answered.

"His name is Dirk Morris ... an underling."

"Dirk Morris," repeated the girl. "It is a pleasant name to the ears. Well ... now that you know the identity of the Ghost, what are you going to do?"

Garroway said slowly, "I am going to do ... nothing. Dirk Morris was put to death almost three weeks ago. The ... the Galactic Ghost is a ghost indeed!"

The girl smiled. "Perhaps," she said thoughtfully. "But a ghost with very tangible body ... and impulses. And, if I am not greatly mistaken, an Achilles' heel. Listen, my father.... I will drive a bargain with you. For a certain price,

I will deliver into your hands this threat to your power."

"Price?" The Overlord stared at her bleakly. "What price do you ask?"

"The life," said the girl, "of the Ghost."

Garroway's brow darkened.

"Have you gone mad?" he demanded harshly. "His life is forfeit the moment my men seize him!"

"But," pointed out the Princess Lenore sagely, "they cannot lay hands on him ... without my help. Come, father ... I, too, can be ruthless in getting that which I desire. Will you give me the man, Dirk Morris, and put an end to these depredations? Or must your fortresses continue to fall because of all on earth, I alone know how this phantom may be caught?"

Garroway's cheeks were mottled with rage; for a moment it seemed he might strike his own daughter.

"You ... you ingrate!" he husked. "You dare bargain with the System's Emperor?"

"I dare bargain," taunted the Princess, "with my own father. And with a badly frightened man."

Garroway fumed at the taunt ... but capitulated, as the Princess had known he must do. He lowered his hands weakly.

"Very well," he said. "I give you your price. Now, what must be done?"

"This—" said the Princess. And for a long time two remarkably similar heads, both in physiognomy and mentality, bent close together in conference....

VI

"Tonight?" asked Dirk Morris. "You're sure, Neil?"

"This very night," swore Neil Hardesty. "At the Palace Royal. I got it on the highest authority. From one of the Imperial Guard, recently converted to our Cause. A grand meeting of the Emperor's strategy Council, summoned to discuss ways and means—" He grinned—"of apprehending the Galactic Ghost."

Dirk Morris smiled, too, though his features were invisible to his friend.

PHANTOM OUT OF TIME

"The Ghost," he promised, "will attend the Council meeting. Neil, send out a hurried summons to all the Group. Tonight may be the night for which we have waited and planned. The situation has finally turned to our advantage. This is the setting we needed to strike our final, and heaviest, blow. A gathering of all Graed Garroway's most trusted lieutenants! What better time to bring an abrupt end to his tyranny?"

"Destruction?" asked Brian Shaughnessey. "You plan to kill them all, Dirk?"

"That is not the best way. Killing would immortalize Garroway and—in the minds of many misguided people—forever brand the Galactic Ghost as an outlaw and murderer. No ... I will not destroy the Overlord. I will make him appear ignominious in the eyes of his subjects ... prove to all men that his vaunted powers are weak and futile. There is no weapon so strong as mirth, no blade so keen as scorn."

Vurrth grunted heavily. "Maybe better you kill, Dirk. No trust Overlord."

"My plans have been successful thus far," pointed out the Voice of Conscience. "Play along with me a little farther. I think the end is in sight. Neil ... be ready to send your forces into the Palace the moment I give the signal."

"Right!"

"And you, Brian ... see that the audiocast stations are controlled by us in time to speed word to the populace that the Emperor has been taken."

"Right, Dirk."

"And you, Vurrth—"

"Me be on hand," growled Vurrth, "to watch Overlord. No like this."

Dirk laughed. "As you will. Well ... until tonight, comrades!"

Again, as oft before during these past weeks, the assembled brothers of the Group sensed the passage of a tingling vibrancy, and knew their leader had gone back to that strange, mysterious other universe which was now his home. Neil issued orders. The Group disbanded.

*

42

Back on Nadron, Dirk Morris sighed and unlimbered himself of the heavy harness which necessity forced his wearing when he made his peregrinations between the two worlds. To the Ptan Slador he said, "Well ... that's all I can do now. I shall try to rest until the hour comes."

"And then?" asked Slador.

"And then," repeated Dirk slowly, "success ... at last. If everything goes well, tonight will mark the beginning of the end. Earth's greatest citadel will fall, carrying with it into destruction not only the Emperor, but all those upon whom the burden of his military power rests.

"With the fall of Earth, half the battle is won. No other planet is so tightly under Garroway's control as ours. With the Overlord imprisoned, the other worlds will burst free of their bondage ... the System will know again the joys of liberty."

Rima said, "Dirk ... you have laid careful plans for tonight? You have plotted every move you will make?"

"Under the circumstances, that is well-nigh impossible. I know only that the Emperor gathers with his staff. I shall have to make my entrance, then decide on the spur of the moment how best to accomplish my aims."

"You are sure—" hesitated the girl—"this is not a trap of some sort?"

"Trap?" Dirk laughed lightly. "How could it be?"

"I don't know. But the Overlord is no fool. He is a ruthless man ... but he is no fool."

"He also," reminded Dirk, "thinks I am dead. The identity of the Galactic Ghost is, to him, a complete mystery. Were he to discover my identity, then perhaps I might have occasion to fear a trap of some sort, for ... as you say ... Garroway is no fool. He would realize, then, that the teleport brought about not death, but some sort of sinister change. But I am sure there is no danger. Ptan Slador ... let us drink to success, and to the final reunion of our freed worlds!"

So they toasted a new life opening to all mankind. And the maiden, Rima, drank the toast with them. But even as she drank, her eyes were grave and thoughtful....

PHANTOM OUT OF TIME

*

Nevertheless, despite his claims of confidence, it was with some slight degree of trepidation that Dirk Morris prepared for his ultimate exploit later that night. This was, he knew, his boldest stroke to date. He had hurled his forces elsewhere with supreme confidence. But always he had avoided too-close contact with Graed Garroway. For in his heart of hearts he agreed with Rima. He knew the Emperor to be, in truth, no fool ... but a cunning adversary of infinite daring and resource.

Still, the die was cast now. The Group's preparations were made; he could not let them down. He must pave the way for the general uprising which would sweep Garroway from power ... or his own scheming into disaster.

Slador and Rima accompanied him to the spot on Nadron where his translation was to take place. It was a tiny wooded glade, bathed in the cool moonlight of the alien planet. In the thickets small night-things chirruped, and from somewhere a sleepy bird sang a listless lullaby. Dirk, standing there breathing the sweet, fresh air of Nadron found it hard to believe that the mere pressure of a switch on his belt would place him on the musty, lower levels of that architectural monstrosity which was the Palace Royal ... a towering structure of numberless stories ... at the very topmost of which would be held the conference he pledged himself to end.

He held out a hand; first Slador, then Rima, gripped it warmly.

"Good luck!" said the Ptan. And Rima added, "We'll be waiting ... and watching!"

Dirk nodded, not daring to trust his thoughts to words, and depressed the switch. As oft before he felt a churning moment of vertigo ... then he stood in a lower corridor of the Palace Royal. Not ten feet distant stood an armed guard. This man stirred restlessly, his head turning as if he felt the electric disturbance of Dirk's entrance. But when his searching eyes found nothing, he returned to the pacing of his post. Dirk slipped past him swiftly, noiselessly, and to the first of the long series of staircases he must negotiate.

The Palace Royal was equipped with elevators, but these he dared not use. The movement of an "empty" elevator would be token enough to the wit-sharpened Palace guards that the dreaded Galactic Ghost was in their midst. So he pressed forward and upward to the heights of the tower.

It was a long climb and a brutal one. The Emperor's palace dwarfed to shame the puny "skyscraper" attempts of ancestors a thousand years removed. Thus it was a weary Dirk Morris who finally attained the topmost flight, and there rested himself briefly before entering the suite which comprised the Overlord's council chamber.

The vagrant thought struck him that the Palace was poorly guarded, considering the chaos into which the Ghost's activities should have thrown the Emperor. But this, he reasoned, might be but another proof of the weakening of Graed Garroway's grip; so undermined was the structure of his empire now that not even in his own bailiwick could he command the meticulous discipline he had heretofore exacted of his hirelings.

Rested at last, he moved toward the massive portal of the council hall. It hung slightly ajar; with no effort he inched it open and eased his still-invisible, but now substantial body through.

His entrance found the Overlord addressing a group seated in a semi-circle about the dais from which Garroway spoke. All backs save that of the Emperor himself were turned to Dirk. He moved forward silently, cautiously.

"—therefore, my lords and generals," the Overlord was saying, "it is vitally necessary that we apprehend this dastard, this criminal, who has so dared attack our government. Never until the so-called Galactic Ghost is captured and put to death will we be free to—"

"—to continue," said Dirk loudly, boldly, "your murderous onslaught against the rights and liberties of freedom loving people! Is that your meaning, Graed Garroway? Then abandon the thought. For truly, tonight your empire crumbles beneath you!"

"*The Ghost!*"

*

The cry lifted in the hall; all heads whirled as one. Eyes opened wide in futile scanning, and jaws fell agape. And of all that vast, terrified assemblage, there was only one who did not freeze with sudden fear. That one was Garroway. Strangely, a smile seized his lips as he cried:

"Yes, the Ghost ... as I had hoped! Guards ... *lights!*"

Instantly the room, which had been cloaked in semi-darkness, blazed with the fury of a thousand beaming flares. And to his horror, Dirk Morris saw....

... not only those who had spun to face him, tight faces wreathed in scowls, hands gripping lethal weapons ... but his own image, reflected a hundred times from every nook and corner of the vast hall! From a hundred mirrors placed to reflect in their revealing rock-quartz surfaces every move he made!

Too late, comprehension dawned upon him! Rima had guessed aright ... this was a trap, ingeniously set for him by the Overlord, and now sprung at the proper moment. The Princess had revealed that which she had seen; the Overlord was clever enough to take advantage of it.

There was but one thing to do, and that quickly! In a trice, Dirk's hand leaped to the control stud on his belt, seeking to depress the switch that would return him to Nadron. But here, too, the Emperor had anticipated his move. His voice again cleft the stark, foreboding silence.

"*Field!*"

And instantly there hummed through the room a shrill, whining current. It took but the split of a second for Dirk Morris to discern its purpose. For when his own hand tightened on the switch ... nothing happened! He did not find himself hurling the vibration-span to the safety of Nadron. He remained where he was, writhing in the coils of an electric agony that coursed through his veins like liquid fire.

It was then the Overlord laughed, his voice a grating triumph.

"You see, Dirk Morris, it is useless! My scientists have probed the secret of your ghostly state ... and you are snared in a net of their devising! Toss down your weapons!"

The grim purpose in his voice left Dirk no choice. Reluctantly he dropped to the floor the weapon with which he had hoped to capture Graed Garroway, stood still as grim-faced guards moved forward to grip him, bundle him to the dais wherefrom watched the smirking Overlord.

The tide was terribly turned. The biter was bitten!

VII

Dirk released the stud, pressure upon which had not brought him the escape he hoped, and gained some consolation in the fact that the pain faded. One thing he would *not* do, he pledged himself, was show fear or hurt before Garroway.

In as level a voice as he could muster he said, "So we meet again, Overlord of scavengers?"

Garroway laughed harshly.

"The trapped rabbit uses strong language still. You have profited little by your experience, I see, Dirk Morris."

"On the contrary," retorted Dirk, "I have profited much. And the measure of my profit lies in the dissolution of your empire ... as you have learned in this past fortnight."

Garroway said, "True, you have caused me trouble. I acknowledge it. But that trouble is ended, now, for I have discovered—at last, but fortunately not too late—the true nature of the machine in which I had thought to execute you. It was *not* a disintegrating machine, but one that distorted the atoms of your body, rendering you invisible."

Dirk's heart leaped; he struggled to maintain the impassive mask which was his face, revealed to the Overlord in a hundred reflecting surfaces of quartz. Then not yet had Garroway learned of the existence of Nadron, of the adjacent universe. That, at least, was something to be thankful for.

He said, "It was a clever trap you set for me, Garroway. You announced a council meeting which you knew I must attend; you surround yourself not with your generals, as was expected, but with guards. You listened to the advice of your daughter, used rock-quartz to make my body visible—"

"—and," added Garroway complacently, "prepared an electric wave-transmitter that disrupted your own instrument, trapped you in our presence, and makes it impossible for you to escape.

PHANTOM OUT OF TIME

"Well—" His voice changed abruptly—"your puny attempt to overthrow me has failed, Morris. As a fighter, I cannot restrain a certain degree of admiration for your effort, but as Emperor of the System, there is one thing I can, and must, do. *Guards—!*"

His voice was a thin snarl.

But as hulking stalwarts moved forward to perform his bidding, another slighter figure hastened before them to confront her parent. The Princess Lenore.

"Wait!" she commanded. "What means this, my parent? Why do you call the guards?"

"Return to your apartment, Lenore!" ordered Garroway sternly. "You have served your purpose. It is not seemly you should witness the judgment on this rebel."

"Have you forgotten your promise?" raged the woman. "You cannot kill this man. You pledged me his life!"

"Forget this foolish whim!" bade her father. "He is but an underling. Surely there are other men—"

"I want this one!" insisted Lenore. For a moment her dark, vivid eyes touched Dirk's with lingering ferocity ... and despite the tenseness of the moment, the peril of his situation, Dirk Morris could not restrain the quick thrill of admiration and ... something else which burned through him. His brain tossed in a turmoil of conflicting emotions. He understood, now, why an ungovernable impulse had caused him to sweep this girl into his arms that night in her apartment. It was because she was ... she was his type of woman! A hard, gallant, ruthless fighting-woman who knew what she wanted and would adopt any measures to get it.

There was Rima on Nadron ... true. He respected her. For her he felt—though he had known her but a short time—a great tenderness and affection. But it was not true love. It was a brotherly feeling; a comfortable confidence in her presence and companionship.

This girl, the Princess Lenore, alone could stir his veins to running fire; she alone quickened a hungry spark within him. It was mad ... it was impossible

48

... but true. He loved—and the knowledge of it struck Dirk Morris with brutally staggering force—he loved an enemy and the daughter of his bitterest foe!

Stranger yet ... she loved him!

Now she was talking again, hurriedly arguing a case to win his life.

"It is not necessary to kill this man, my parent. It would be folly to do so. Think! On all this world ... in all this universe ... there are few men worthy of the name of *man*! Your court is a *melange* of smirking nincompoops and weaklings. Who amongst them can match in strength and vigor the spirit of Dirk Morris? Which can compare with him in audacity and daring?"

"That," responded her father darkly, "is why he must die. I cannot allow so dangerous a foe to live—"

"No? Have you forgotten the medical science of which your attendants are capable? Think, my father ... were it not better to make slight alterations in this man's brain, converting him to a true and faithful servant, than to destroy forever the bravery in his heart?"

The words struck home. Garroway frowned thoughtfully.

"It is true," he mused. "A slight operation ... a period in the Mental Clinic to erase from his brain-passage all thoughts of rebellion ... would make him a new man. But it is too great a chance. Were anything to go wrong—"

The Princess Lenore gazed at him scornfully.

"I see. Very well, then—" With slow, deliberate movements she reached up, stripped from her raven hair the glittering imperial emblem which designated her a member of the Family Royal—"if such must be your decision, so be it! But I ... I shall no longer confess myself a Garroway. If the word of the Emperor is so lightly to be given...."

And this time she was triumphant. Her scorn hit the Overlord in his one most vulnerable spot ... his colossal vanity. His dark eyes flamed with petulance. He snarled, "Oh, let be! No man shall say the Overlord retracted a pledge. If you must have this man—" He turned to Morris—"Well, what say *you*, rebel? Are you too proud to buy your life at the expense of rebellion? Or will you accept life at the price of a new existence of loyalty ... to me?"

PHANTOM OUT OF TIME

*

Dirk wavered, sorely tempted. Until this moment his life had been consecrated to a single Cause ... the overthrow of Garroway's cruel empire. But now, suddenly, strangely, singingly, had entered into it another influence ... love for a woman of matchless courage and beauty.

His attempts to destroy Garroway had failed. He was hopelessly ensnared, his cohorts could not save him. Years might pass before another Dirk Morris arose to lead malcontents in rebellion. Neil Hardesty was a good man, a strong and faithful friend ... but he lacked the spark of genius that leads lost causes to success.

Perhaps it would be better, in the long run, to accept defeat ... and in accepting it, accept also such share of happiness as this world had to offer. As the mate of Lenore he would live a new life, all rebellious thoughts exiled from his brain by the surgery of Garroway's physicians....

So he hesitated, and for those tense moments the fate of a world hung in the balance. But then ... honor won! With infinite sadness, but with courage too, Dirk Morris made his answer. It was symbolic that he made it to the Princess.

"I am sorry, my Princess," he said quietly. "I know a great wonder, and a great pride, that you have made this plea for me. But ... I cannot accept life on such terms. For me there is but one clear and unavoidable path ... to go on. This path I must choose to glory or ... the grave."

"Don't be a fool!" cried the girl. "Don't you see you can gain nothing by this gesture. You have no choice!"

Her words were sharp ... but her voice was fearful. Dirk, recognized this as he said, still softly, "Yes, that, too, I see. And, believe me, Princess, I am deeply sorry. But I have made my choice."

For an instant that seemed eternities the Princess Lenore, she who had until a fortnight since known passion for nothing save costly baubles, stared into Dirk's eyes. Then a little sob broke from her lips, and she turned away.

And the Emperor nodded.

"Guards!" he said. "Take this man—"

50

NELSON S. BOND

It was a command that was never obeyed ... an order never completed! For at that moment came interruption in the form of a violent blast that shook the entire council hall as a thatched shack trembles in a cyclone's wake. A column of living fire blossomed in the room; eyes burned and eardrums throbbed to see and hear the tingling of an unleashed and unguessable *force* turned loose in their midst.

And in the heart of this column, loose-girt in shining white, radiant as a goddess, but calm with the ominous quiet of powers unfathomable ... stood the girl, *Rima of Nadron!*

*

It was Morris who first recovered sufficiently from the unexpected appearance to make a movement. A cry broke from his lips, "*Rima!*" He moved toward the girl. But her voice lifted in crisp warning.

"Back, Dirk! To touch this flame means death!"

Her words stopped not only Morris, but a group of the Imperial Guards who, as one, had now spun toward the visitant. They faltered, stopped dead in their tracks and turned to the Overlord for guidance.

Graed Garroway's black eyebrows were knit with rage and bafflement. He demanded hoarsely, "Who is this woman? And whence comes she, that she dares enter the stronghold of the Emperor?"

It was incredible how forceful could be the tones of Rima. Her voice was dulcet sweet, but carried conviction.

"I am of a race that ruled this world before your ilk was spawned, Black Garroway ... a race whose least remembered knowledge so surpasses your own that you are as pawns with which we play at will.

"I came because the evil in your heart has inspired you to do a great wrong ... a wrong upon mankind that we, who once loved Earth, can neither condone nor allow. I came to free Dirk Morris, and to free Earth of a tyrant.

"Dirk ... bid the Emperor step from his dais. He no longer rules this city or this System."

"No longer rules—" choked Garroway.

"The city has fallen," said Rima. "While in this tower you plotted for the life of a rebel leader, you have lost an empire. Listen ... or better yet, turn on your visi-screens. Therein you will see I speak the truth."

In sudden, fumbling haste Graed Garroway turned to a vision-unit set in the auditorium wall. Instantly a section of the capital city sprawled before the gaze of those assembled. It was as Rima had foretold. No matter where the dial was swung, there reflected the same scene: people leaping, laughing, rejoicing in the streets ... marching in vast, inchoate crowds, singing and cheering. Here and there were grisly evidences of the reason for their rejoicing ... a knot of tumbled bodies garbed in the uniform of Garroway's forces ... a burning pyre which had been an Imperial blockhouse ... a torn, stained militiaman's cap lying in a gutter.

And now, to further the evidence, came the sound of voices, running footsteps, through the tower itself. And into the council hall flooded a host of jubilant freedmen, led by a trio at sight of whom Dirk's heart filled with gladness. The gigantic Vurrth, grinning from ear to ear and wearing a jacket snatched from a fallen foe ... a jacket that had ripped up the back under the strain of the Venusian's mighty muscles. Brian Shaughnessey, bellowing loud greetings. Neil Hardesty, grave and quiet as ever, even in this hour of triumph, as he spoke to his leader.

"It is over, Dirk. You have succeeded here, too?"

Dirk said ruefully, "I have succeeded, yes. But it was not of my doing. Rima—"

"He has succeeded," interrupted the Nadronian girl. "The Emperor is deposed."

Neil said gratefully, "We awaited your signal, Dirk. When it did not come we grew anxious. Then Rima—" For an instant his eyes sought those of the alien girl, and there was a curious humility in them, an almost worshipful admiration—"then Rima came to us; told us the hour had struck. We issued our rallying cry. It ... it was easier than we had dared hope. The city was like a ripe plum, ready for our taking. At every street-corner new hordes joined us. Even Garroway's hirelings abandoned their old leaders to follow the standard of the fabulous Galactic Ghost."

"Thus, you see," said Rima so softly that only Dirk could hear her, "you *did* succeed, Dirk Morris. It was the Ghost whose spirit forged this rebellion. I but stepped in when the moment needed me."

*

Garroway, who had been standing at the vision plate, staring as a man transfixed at the image of his own downfall, now turned to his destroyers. His dark eyes were haggard, his sagging jowls suddenly no longer the harsh features of a ruler, but those of a defeated old man. He whispered:

"This, then, is the end? Very well—" A burst of his former defiance flamed in him. He forced a laugh. "You have won, Dirk Morris. And the death I promised you lies in store for me? Well ... so be it. It has been a long game, but one worth the playing. Of one thing you cannot rob me ... the memory that once I ruled the mightiest empire known to man."

But again it was Rima who spoke. Her voice was like a crystal bell.

"Not death, Graed Garroway. It is the right of none to judge that ultimate penalty on another. *Exile* shall be your fate. Those who know your system better than I shall decide which planet ... or planetoid far removed from Earth ... shall be your final refuge.

"Neil Hardesty—" She turned to the listening captain—"send him away. Your new government shall sit in judgment on him later."

Hardesty nodded, motioned to Shaughnessey, and the erstwhile Overlord was led away. With him were herded from the room, none too gently, those who had been his companions in the attempt to trap Dirk. Within a matter of minutes the hall was cleared save for a handful: Dirk and Rima, in her glowing pillar of flame; Hardesty, the Princess Lenore.

In the Princess' eyes glittered a great defiance and a great sorrow. She asked, "And I? I join my father in exile?"

Rima looked at Dirk.

"Well, Dirk Morris?" she asked.

Dirk's throat was dry, his mind confusion. He said, "Must ... must I, then, be the one to judge, Rima? She saved my life ... or tried to. Were it not for her—"

PHANTOM OUT OF TIME

Rima said gently, "You love her. Isn't that what you mean, Dirk?"

Dirk's head turned slowly; his eyes met those of the Princess Lenore. And what he found there forced the answer from his lips.

"Yes, Rima. May the gods help me ... I love her."

"That," said the Nadronian girl, "I know. And this also I know ... that she loves you. Does she love you enough to join you in the new world which is the only one whereon you now can live? Enough to join you on Nadron?"

It was Lenore who answered that question. She said simply, "I do not understand your meaning, woman who dwells in a column of flame ... but this much I *do* know. Where Dirk Morris dwells, there would I dwell also."

Rima nodded, satisfied.

"That, too, I had expected. It is well. She will make you a good mate, Dirk Morris. I wish—" There was a strange catch in her voice, a catch clenched teeth upon her lower lip could not quite stifle—"I wish you ... much joy ... in my lost, beloved homeland—"

Dirk stared at her aghast, uncomprehending. "Rima!" he cried. "Lost homeland? I don't understand—"

The maid of Nadron smiled wanly. Her voice, when she spoke, was infinitely gentle.

"Surely *you* should know, Dirk Morris, that one cannot pass with impunity from one universe of vibration to another?"

Dirk said, "You mean that you, as I did, have become a ... a wraith to your own world? That henceforth you have no true existence on Nadron, as I none on Earth?"

Rima nodded quietly, sadly.

"But then," stammered Dirk, "if not on Nadron, where *is* your new plane of existence?" A hope caught and tugged at his heart. "Earth, perhaps? Our planet will become your new world?"

*

Rima shook her head. "No, Dirk Morris. The atomic pathway of Space-Time winds ever upward ... not downward to a lower vibrational plane. When this protective shield, which already wanes—" She glanced with a swift, despairing apprehension as the iridescence dulled, and a crepuscular wavering dimmed its outlines—"When this shield wanes, I shall move ... forward to a bourne I cannot guess. A better world, perhaps, or ... a worse—"

"No!" cried Dirk. He started forward, but within the blazing column a white arm rose in stern command.

"No farther, Dirk. To touch this field means death!"

"Rima!" cried Dick huskily. "Rima, you shouldn't have done this. It wasn't required of you!"

"The quest of liberty," said the girl softly, "is the quest of all men, all women, everywhere. I was watching your progress, Dirk. When I saw you had been trapped, I knew someone must come to your aid, someone must carry out the plans you had so carefully laid.

"My father was too old. The journey between our two worlds is ... well, not without pain. So—" The girl smiled—"I came."

"You sacrificed yourself," cried Dirk humbly, "for us. It is too much. Earth can never repay you, Rima."

"I was repaid when you refused life at the expense of your own honor, Dirk. Now it is done I can tell you that on your decision at that moment rested the future fate of Earth. We of Nadron have ever hesitated in dabbling in the affairs of others. Had you proved unworthy of our aid in that moment of trial. I would not have made the journey.

"And now—" There flickered in her eyes a shadow of thin, wondering fear as the veil of flame about her seemed to shudder—"the time has come for ... parting—"

"No!" shouted Dirk, as if by the very strength of his cry he could withhold the inexorable. "No, Rima! Don't—"

His cry ended in a little moan. For at that moment the shimmering column trembled and ... vanished like the flame of a snuffed candle. The last vision of Rima to be burned forevermore upon the retina of Dirk Morris' memory was that of a slim and gallant goddess, whiteclad, lifting a soft arm in salute ... and farewell.

Then ... nothing.

PHANTOM OUT OF TIME

*

Dirk turned away, shaken. He whispered, "Gone! Rima ... gone ... no one knows where—"

Lenore said soberly, "*She* loved you, too, Dirk."

"No. She never loved me. Not as I love you ... not as you love me—"

"It was a different kind of love," said the princess.

"I will find her!" vowed Dirk brokenly.

Lenore moved to his side quietly; the warmth of her beside him like the courage of a voice in the wilderness.

"You and I," she breathed, "together, Dirk."

And suddenly, though there stretched before him a new and greater quest than that recently acquitted, Dirk was consumed with a vast impatience to know again the lips of the girl whose nearness was a heady wine, challenging him to dare any danger. He turned to Lenore.

"Together," he agreed. "But first I must return to Nadron to lay the plans. You ... you will come soon, my Princess?"

"Soon," she promised. "Soon. But, first—"

She moved toward his voice. If she closed her eyes, she could not tell it was invisible arms that held her close, nor invisible lips that quickened upon her own....

www.ingramcontent.com/pod-product-compliance
Lightning Source LLC
Chambersburg PA
CBHW050912120626
46552CB00004B/1528